This book belongs to

_____

For Cindy—who doesn't even like turkey!
— B.G.F.

For the Sarkis family, dear friends all, with love.
— L.McQ.

Library of Congress Cataloging-in-Publication Data is available.

2 4 6 8 10 9 7 5 3 1

Published by Sterling Publishing Co., Inc. 387 Park Avenue South, New York, NY 10016
Text copyright © 2005 by Bernette G. Ford
Illustrations copyright © 2005 by Lucinda McQueen

The text for this book was adapted from a popular children's song believed to be in the public domain. Every effort has been made to trace the ownership of any copyrighted material. In the event of a question arising as to its use, the author and the publisher, while expressing regret for any inadvertent error, will be happy to make the necessary correction in future printings.

Designed and produced for Sterling by COLOR-BRIDGE BOOKS, LLC, Brooklyn, NY

Distributed in Canada by Sterling Publishing
c/o Canadian Manda Group, 165 Dufferin Street
Toronto, Ontario, Canada M6K 3H6
Distributed in Great Britain and Europe by Chris Lloyd at Orca Book Services,
Stanley House, Fleets Lane, Poole BH15 3AJ, England
Distributed in Australia by Capricorn Link (Australia) Pty. Ltd.
P.O. Box 704, Windsor, NSW 2756, Australia

Sterling ISBN 1-4027-2039-4

Albuquerque Turkey

(Sung to the tune of "Oh, My Darlin', Clementine")

Adapted by B. G. Ford · Illustrated by Lucinda McQueen

Sterling Publishing Co., Inc.
New York

Albuquerque is a turkey
And he's feathered
And he's fine,

And he wobbles
And he gobbles
And he's absolutely mine.

He's the best pet
That you can get,
Better than a dog or cat.

He's my Albuquerque Turkey,
And I'm awfully proud of that.

Oh, he wobbles
And he gobbles

And he follows me all day . . .

To the market . . .

To the grocer . . .

Then back home—
He knows the way.

Wednesday morning
I was baking—

Apple pie,
And pumpkin, too.

When I started
Peeling onions,
Albuquerque cried,
"Boo-hoo!"

"You're not using those for stuffing?!"

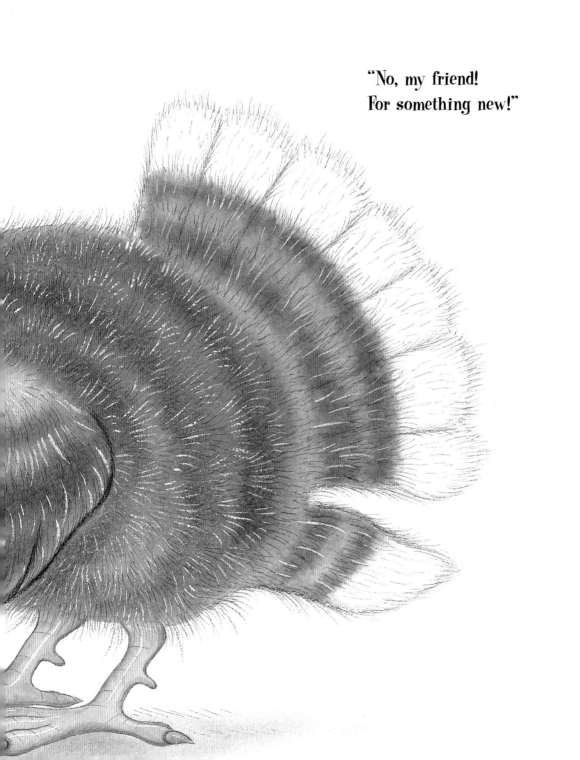

"No, my friend!
For something new!"

Oh, he wobbles
And he gobbles
And he follows me once more . . .

To the store for eggs and spices—
Then back home,
Just like before.

Now my Albuquerque Turkey
Is all safely tucked in bed.
'Cause for our Thanksgiving dinner . . .

We have Egg Foo Yong instead.